*Ivan and the
informer*

Myrna Grant

Ivan and the informer

KINGSWAY PUBLICATIONS
EASTBOURNE

© Tyndale House Publishers Inc 1974 and 1977
Wheaton, Illinois, USA.

First British edition 1978

ISBN 0 86065 028 6

Illustrated by Jos. E. DeVelasco

Printed in Great Britain for
KINGSWAY PUBLICATIONS LTD
Lottbridge Drove, Eastbourne, E. Sussex BN23 6NT by
Hunt Barnard Printing Ltd, Aylesbury, Bucks.

Contents

*For Chris,
Sue, Drew,
and Jenni
with love
and appreciation*

The threat

Ivan Nazaroff strode along the snow-filled Moscow street, trying hard to pretend that nothing had happened. Behind him, he could hear the running footsteps of his sister, Katya. Her heavy boots were thudding through snow that had been falling all day and was swirling like clouds of smoke around the hunched and hurrying people.

'Ivan! Wait for me!'

Ivan wondered how many times he had heard that call. Sometimes it was tiresome to be always waiting for a ten-year-old sister, two whole years younger than he. Today it was worse than tiresome. He wanted to think.

Katya's face was bright with cold as she laid a thickly-gloved hand on Ivan's coat sleeve to steady herself and catch her breath. 'The bus was so crowded, I almost missed getting off,' she gasped. 'Didn't you wonder where I was?'

Ivan marched on ahead, hoping his sister would not notice that he was upset. 'Certainly not. You're much too old to have a brother leading you around. Besides, I saw you shoving your way off the bus.'

Katya glanced quickly at her brother's stern face. 'Why was Boris Petrovich waiting for you after school today?' She asked the question with a stab of fear. She knew Boris had just had his fifteenth birthday and was a new member of the Komsomol, the communist youth organisation.

A gust of wind flung itself at the children, making them stagger against its force. Ivan fought ahead, pushing out his anger at Boris. He was grateful that the wind made it impossible to answer Katya.

But the turning of the corner gave them relief from the wind, and Katya, with her usual persistence, repeated the question.

'Same as always,' Ivan finally answered. 'He knows I'm a Christian. He likes to make fun of me.'

'But it wasn't the same,' Katya retorted, her eyebrows tense with concern. 'I saw him pushing you. He's a bully.'

Ivan sighed. Katya had a way of persisting in her questions until she finally got the whole story, no matter what. 'He said that as a Komsomol member he has a responsibility to convince me that Christianity is old-fashioned superstition. I told him I didn't have to listen to him, but he thinks he can make me.'

'How will he make you?' The wind almost carried off Katya's words. 'He can't *make* you listen!'

Ivan was trying not to think about it, let alone talk about it. But Katya's glance was insistent. 'He's on the ice hockey team. The others know I'm a believer and say nothing. The coach knows, but he's interested in a good team and I'm a good player. But if Boris protests about my being on the team, the coach will have to remove me. After all, the team is for the Young Pioneers, and believers don't belong to that!'

'But you have worked so hard! And it's such an honour to be chosen for the team. He's horrid!' Katya flung the words out with such indignation that an old woman, bent double as she slowly shovelled snow, stiffly raised her head and glanced briefly at Katya.

'We had an argument. I walked away. He would have come after me, but his bus was coming. He said he would be waiting for me after school tomorrow. He means to fight me.'

Ivan pulled open the heavy door of the block of flats for his sister. It was a great relief to be in the long hallway and out of the wind and snow. He spoke quietly. 'Say nothing of this to Mum, Katya. We don't want to worry her.'

The wonderful smell of borscht greeted them as they entered their apartment.

'Mum, we're home!' Katya called, pulling off her boots with stiff fingers. Ivan sat down at the large table in the centre of the living room, smiling as his mother bent to kiss him.

'What a cold day, children!' she exclaimed. 'I have some hot tea ready for you. Katya, get the pot from the kitchen, please, and I'll bring out the glasses.'

Ivan was glad this was a day his mother was home early from her job at the factory. He liked to smell the thick borscht soup already hot and to watch her steady hands laying out glasses and spoons and pouring the tea.

The children sat quietly, breathing the steam from the hot tea and feeling it warm their icy faces. Mother sat at the table with them, mending silently and smiling when she glanced at the two children. Katya sipped her tea slowly. She wanted to make it last, but Ivan was already beginning his homework, his glass set carefully beside his book.

It would be at least an hour, Ivan knew, before Father returned from his factory job, and in that hour

Ivan could get a good start on what he had to complete for school tomorrow.

A good feeling settled upon Ivan. Boris's threats seemed far away. The tension of being the only believer in his classroom, the only one not to wear proudly the red neck scarf of the communist Young Pioneers, seemed eased. What if the others made fun of him? Here in this room, with the tea still warming him and the quiet face of his mother bending over her sewing, the difficulties at school subsided. Ivan raised his head from his book to smile at Katya. He was sorry he had been so irritated with her after school. But as he glanced up, the soft lace curtains at the window across the room suddenly lifted as a blast of cold air swept in from the open front door. He turned in his chair with astonishment.

Dad in trouble

'Dad! What are you doing home so early from your job?' Ivan jumped to his feet and anxiously took his father's heavy coat and hung it on the hook by the door.

'Dad, are you ill?' Ivan persisted. Dad sank wearily into his chair.

'Oh, no, son! I'm not ill.' He smiled to relieve the family's concern. 'It's nothing *so* bad. I was asked to leave my job at the factory. I am to report to the supervisor in the morning.'

Mum's voice was filled with dismay. 'But why?'

Dad shrugged. 'Last week, one of the men beside me on the assembly line was asking me about Christian beliefs. It was a wonderful conversation.'

'But Sergei, you know you must not speak about religion at the factory.'

'I was answering his questions. That is permitted by our Soviet law.'

Katya burst out indignantly, 'It's *supposed* to be permitted.'

'He was my friend.'

Mum went to the window and stared out. The room was quiet. 'Believers cannot trust friends in Russia.' The children could hear a tinge of weariness in her voice. 'So often such people are only police informers, wanting to cause trouble.'

The face of Boris Petrovich suddenly appeared in Ivan's mind. A tight feeling of fear returned to his chest, and he looked down at his school book still open on the table.

'We have other believers for friends, Mum,' Ivan reminded her gently.

Mum turned from the window with a smile. 'Of course! This is not so bad. Your father will have an opportunity in the morning to explain to the supervisor that he was only answering his comrade's questions.' Mum gave Dad a warm hug.

Dad pulled Mum to the chair beside him and held her hand. 'It is good for us to pray about all this.'

Ivan and Katya nodded eagerly and bowed their heads as Dad began. 'Thanksgiving and praise to Almighty God, that I am counted worthy to bear this small concern for the sake of Jesus. Praise for the love of God, that can reach even to my supervisor. Praise for the forgiveness of God, that can give new life to the worker who reported me.'

A feeling of sweetness touched Ivan, as it had many times before in prayer.

'Bring glory to the name of Jesus,' Mum prayed.

Ivan silently agreed, and within himself he added, *Even through me, Lord, if you want. Even through me.*

Mum gave Katya a playful spank. 'Come! Let's set the table for supper!'

'Yes! Borscht!' Ivan declared enthusiastically. 'It smells so good, Mum.'

Dad inhaled deeply. 'It's the best in Moscow, Ivan. Your Mum made it.'

'I peeled the beets!' Katya shook out the tablecloth.

'And I went to the shop especially for the sour cream. You should have seen all the queues today. It was no fun, I tell you! Waiting all that time just for sour cream!'

Dad tugged teasingly at the bow that caught Katya's two brown braids in a pretty loop at the back of her head. 'Someday you will be as fine a cook as your Mum, Katychka. Keep peeling the beets!'

They all laughed, Ivan louder than the rest.

It had been cold all day in the classroom, and Ivan wrapped his sweater tightly around himself and folded his arms, hugging himself for warmth. Usually he loved history, but today it was hard to listen to his teacher, Sophia Kutskova. His mind was on his father's factory and what had happened at Dad's meeting with the supervisor. Sophia Kutskova was talking about the examinations which she had just handed back.

'Our leader, Lenin, would have been proud of your work, students. You have mastered some rather lengthy sections of Soviet history, and I, too, am pleased. It is important that you should be able to follow the development of all that went into our glorious revolution.'

The clock on the wall reminded Ivan that in a few minutes, school would be over, and perhaps he would have to confront Boris. He tried harder to concentrate on what his teacher was saying.

'In a very few years, many of you students will be proud to be in the Komsomol.' Sophia Kutskova's eyes rested for an instant on Ivan, then moved away. 'You will be happy, then, to have studied so diligently. Your history will mean even more to you when you all take your places in the service of your country in the Young

2

Communist League.' She paused. 'Now you are dismissed.'

Ivan gathered his books up quickly. *If only Katya is ready, perhaps we can hurry and avoid Boris,* he thought. He was startled to hear his teacher calling his name.

'Ivan Nazaroff, stay back. I wish to speak to you.'

Ivan hurried to the front of the room. His teacher smiled as she beckoned him to sit down. She glanced at the open grade book on her desk. 'You did well on your history examination.'

Ivan returned his teacher's smile. 'Thank you, Sophia Kutskova. I like history very much.'

'I confess, I do not understand your behaviour.' The teacher looked suddenly grave.

Ivan felt a pang of guilt. He tried to think what he could have done.

'You excel in history,' Sophia Kutskova continued. 'I sense in you a deep stirring of love for Mother Russia. And yet you will not wear the red neck scarf that shows you to be a loyal communist Young Pioneer.'

'I'm sorry, Sophia Kutskova.'

'We have talked together many times. You understand so much, Ivan. It makes me sorry to see you stubborn and set against me.'

Ivan flushed. A flutter of fear tightened his voice. 'I am not against *you*, Sophia Kutskova.'

'Your parents are lost in the past. If they were not, they would know how corrupt and imperialistic their religious ideas are. They are clinging ignorantly to ideas that were swept away with the czars. But you are young, Ivan, and have before you the possibility of a great education.'

His teacher looked at Ivan expectantly. When he did

not reply, she continued with a lecture Ivan had heard many times before, from many teachers.

'Why can you not see that you are throwing away your future for nothing? In years to come, no university will admit you if you cling to these fanatical ideas. I implore you to think about your future.' Once again his teacher paused.

This time Ivan knew he must answer. 'I do think about it, Sophia Kutskova.'

The teacher smiled warmly. 'Good. Then you will see that these uncultured ideas, this unscientific religious superstition, cannot be for a young and progressive Soviet youth like you. There is nothing ahead for you but trouble and suffering if you cling to religion.'

She stood up, still smiling. Ivan stood also and picked up his books. 'Thank you, Sophia Kutskova. I know you have my interests at heart.'

The teacher laid her small hand on his shoulder. 'Of course I do.' She paused and looked warningly at him. 'And do you think it is easy for me to have one student in my class, as late in the year as this, who still refuses to wear the red scarf?'

A new job

Ivan walked slowly, trying to make the short block between bus stop and home last as long as possible. Feelings of relief and dread were struggling in his mind.

He was relieved that Boris had not carried out his threat to fight him after school. Even the ice hockey practice today had been uneventful, although since Boris was the oldest boy on the team, his influence with the coach worried Ivan. And today Boris had seemed to make as much of that relationship as possible. Time and again he had skated up to the coach, resting his stiffly-gloved hand on the coach's shoulder, suggesting plays, making little jokes, or listening to some confidence of the coach and nodding his head in agreement. But nothing had been said about Ivan.

All the same, Ivan's steps were slow with dread. Perhaps Boris and his threats were unimportant, but what had happened to his father today at the meeting with his supervisor was important!

There was no good smell of borscht today as Ivan opened the door of the flat. The tearful face of Katya was the first thing he saw. Ivan's heart sank.

Her voice was thick from crying. 'Ivan! Where have you been? Dad has been at the police station all day. Mum went there when I got home from school, to see if she could find out anything.' Katya hunched miserably in the corner of a big chair. Her schoolbooks were unopened on the table across the room.

'I was at ice hockey practice.' Ivan unwound his knitted scarf and sat on the arm of Katya's chair.

'Everything is wrong, Ivan. I'm so worried about Dad. And hardly anyone in my class will be friends with me. They think I am stupid to believe in God. I want to have friends like everyone else.'

Ivan awkwardly handed her his handkerchief. 'You have Christian friends,' he offered, trying to be helpful.

'If I don't mind never seeing them!' Katya blew her nose loudly. 'How often can we meet, anyway? It has to be someone's wedding or birthday or funeral, because believers have to get permission to meet in homes. I want to be with a lot of friends, all together, and without worrying about the police!' She blew her nose again and began to feel better.

Ivan was thinking that perhaps they ought to pray for Dad, but before he could suggest it, the door swiftly opened and their parents hurried into the room, cold from the walk from the police station.

It had not been a bad time, really, Dad said cheerfully. The police had asked why he was trying to influence fellow workers to become believers. Dad had explained that he had only been answering his fellow worker's questions, and this was allowed by law.

Mum blew into the hot glass of pale tea that Katya had brought to warm her. 'Then they brought the superintendent from the factory, and he accused your father of laziness and stealing!'

Dad continued unlacing his heavy work boots. 'We should laugh, Natasha. So many of the men take things from the factory – a small tool, or some wood. The

21

superintendent himself has carried off enough supplies to begin a small shop of his own. And *he* tells the police that *I* have been stealing.'

Mum's voice was unsteady. 'And to think you have never stolen so much as a minute from the factory!'

'But what about your job, Dad?' Ivan was impatient to get to the outcome.

'It's not so bad. Not nearly so bad as it could be. A new job, but I'll be home every night. I have been assigned to the State Collective Farm Number 46, outside Moscow.'

Katya jumped up and stamped her foot. Her dark eyes were flashing. 'A farm worker! Oh! To do nothing wrong! To be honest and good, and to be punished! How glorious is our Mother Russia!'

Mum placed a firm hand on Katya's arm. 'Katya! I have spoken to you before about this. You must guard your thoughts and your tongue. You know the danger in speaking carelessly.'

But Katya was still angry. 'Perhaps Ivan is an informer? You think he will tell what I said?'

'It is the habit of thought and speech that I fear,' Mum replied sternly. 'You must learn to discipline your thoughts!' She stared at Katya as if she would say more and then sighed. 'You children have homework to do, and I have supper to prepare. Let's talk no more about this.'

Later that night, Ivan lay awake in bed. The moon shone through the lace curtains at the window. His parents had talked and prayed long into the night, and the drone of their voices had made him drowsy. But now they were silent, and Ivan propped himself up on his elbow and looked at the drifting moon.

It *was* unjust that his father, a trained factory worker,

was assigned to a farm. His father had only answered a fellow worker's questions about Christianity. But the supervisor disliked believers and had chosen to report Dad, and the police had chosen to pretend to believe the lie about Dad's stealing. The police, the supervisor, and Dad all knew that the real reason Dad was being sent to the farm was to make life difficult for him because he was a believer.

Sophia Kutskova's words rang in Ivan's memory. *There is nothing ahead for you but trouble and suffering, if you cling to religion.*

The moon slipped behind a dense cloud, plunging the room into darkness. A few faint stars, not visible before, came into view.

How strange that simply to believe in God could cause such troubles. For as long as he could remember, Ivan had known God existed. He could not imagine 'changing his mind' to say that there was no God. A person had only to look at the sky to know the wonder of God's creation !

But commitment to Jesus had not come easily to Ivan. When he had become old enough to understand the cost of being a believer, he had been afraid. Life was too exciting, too full of possibilities, to choose a life that would close so many important doors. Ivan smiled at the emerging moon as he remembered his determination to resist the call of Jesus Christ. It seemed so long ago.

His conversion had been simple, really. Ivan remembered walking in the forest in the spring, in a world of green light and damp freshness. When he had gone into the forest, he had not been a Christian. When he had come out, he was. He tried to bring back what had happened to him in that walk, but it was a blur. His mind had been pulling in all directions; he remembered that. Then there had been a long time spent sitting against a tree. There had been an inner listening to some Bible verses Mum had taught him. There had been an inner argument, too. Then a warm sense of a Presence had come over him, and a word, 'Come!' echoed in his heart. He had walked out of the forest with Christ. That part he remembered. And how Dad had cried for joy! Dad!

Ivan was fully awake now! How could he have lain, half-dreaming, forgetful of what awaited his father in the morning? Was it not a disgrace that a skilled factory worker would dig and carry on a farm? Dad would have to leave Moscow on the earliest possible train and return to the apartment late. Was this not unjust? Ivan lay back on his pillow, staring at the ceiling. Morning would be a long time in coming.

A secret meeting

The argument had started slowly. Ivan had not meant to quarrel with Dad. In fact, he had wanted to help him in some way. Ivan could see how tired and discouraged he was feeling after his first long day on the collective farm.

'Never mind, Natasha,' Dad had said to Mum. 'Was not our Lord falsely accused? It is an honour to suffer for his sake.'

It was not the words that had made Ivan feel a surge of love for his father. It was the playful way Dad had smiled, as if comparing himself to the Saviour were a gentle kind of joke.

Dad had eaten his supper hungrily, but without talking. When it was over, he called Ivan away from the last pages of his homework, talking softly because Katya was already in bed.

'You were planning, son, on meeting some of your friends this Sunday?'

Ivan had answered happily. It was his friend Alexi's birthday, and a perfect time for a few Christian boys to gather at Alexi's home without raising suspicion. But Dad had been hesitant.

'Perhaps it would be best, this time, not to go. My trouble with the police –'

Ivan could tell by Mum's face that she agreed. She was clearing away Dad's dinner plate and paused to listen to the conversation.

'But Dad! No! I promised I would go. It is the only chance we boys have to be together and talk freely as believers. They will think I am afraid if I don't go. They'll know you have been sent to the collective farm.'

Dad observed that it was not quite as important what one's friends thought as what the police thought. He explained again how careful Christians had to be not to draw attention to themselves in any way. But Ivan pleaded all the harder to be allowed to go. In the end, Dad had given permission.

'Come in, Ivan! You're covered with snow!' With the exuberance of a boy newly turned fourteen, Alexi flung open the door. His high cheekbones were flushed with colour, and his fair hair had been carefully combed for the occasion.

'Happy birthday, Alexi!' Ivan embraced his friend warmly, in the Russian manner. 'My mother sends these biscuits.'

'Thank you!' Alexi slammed the door hard, oblivious to the amusement of the other guests. 'Off with your coat and boots, Ivan. You look frozen.'

He held the biscuits aloft, bearing them to the table with a flourish. Two boys, both older than Ivan, sat watching Ivan's entrance with smiles of pleasure. At the same time they followed with keen interest the path of the biscuits through the air.

'These we shall have with tea,' Alexi declared. 'And the little cakes Mother made for us.'

'A feast!' Pyotr Kachenko was tall for his age, and sturdy. 'Good peasant stock,' he said to himself with satisfaction, and whether it was his height or his peasant stock that provided him with an astonishing appetite, no one knew.

But Alexi whisked the biscuits to a safe distance, placing them in front of Fyodor Sakovich. Fyodor was Pyotr's opposite. Small for fifteen, and slight of build, he was the pride of his family because of his athletic ability and excellent grades at school. With a grin, he pushed the biscuits even farther down the table, away from Pyotr's enthusiasm, meanwhile greeting Ivan with a wave of his free hand.

Alexi emerged from the kitchen, carrying a small tea tray clinking with glasses. On a side table in the room sat a brass samovar, the family's prized possession. Its surface was beaded with steam from the scalding water inside. With gusto, Alexi began making the tea and handing the glasses to his friends.

'Looks more like a real birthday party this way! It's always best to be on the safe side, brothers!'

Ivan smiled at his friend. 'It *is* a birthday party, Alexi. I do wish you many years to come.'

The other boys added their greetings until Alexi was beaming with embarrassed pleasure and passing the cakes and biscuits insistently, even though he had secretly hoped to have some left over for bedtime.

Today, in preparation for the birthday, Alexi had copied down some Scripture from a recent overseas radio broadcast. With a flourish of triumph, he pulled a folded paper out of his pocket.

'This Scripture I have is from Jeremiah!' He opened the paper and laid it carefully on the table in front of him. 'Some of it in the middle I missed, because Masha fell out of bed and made a great racket and I couldn't hear.'

Pyotr threw back his head and laughed loudly. 'Radios should come with ropes for tying up little sisters! In my case, *chains* for our Sonya!' The exploits of Pyotr's tiny sister were notorious. 'But never mind, let's get on with what you have.'

Soon the boys were absorbed in the words of Alexi's paper. Then they talked quietly together about what must be left behind when one follows Christ.

Pyotr's merry eyes became grave when he talked about his dream of continuing his piano lessons. 'My teacher says I'm good enough to play here in Moscow someday, if I could keep on. But of course, I am not a member of the Komsomol, so advanced lessons are impossible.'

'It's sports that I miss.' Fyodor spoke in a low voice. The boys knew how much gymnastics meant to him.

But Fyodor brightened and smiled with a shrug. 'Once when I was small, I was in a physical culture show at Dynamo Stadium. That's something to remember! There were hundreds of us on the field, and when we finished, a great curtain of water jets shot to the sky. It was wonderful! But of course, the Organisation of Sports Societies does not permit entrance to anyone not in the Komsomol. Now that I am fifteen and should have joined, that is over for me.'

'But the Lord will repay you, Fyodor,' Alexi reminded him softly.

'No question of that. But it's hard.'

As the youngest boy in the group, Ivan said little. It was enough to be with Christian friends, feeling the warmth of their mutual affection and concerns. The awkward, tight feeling that sometimes closed in on him at school was completely gone. He loved to bend his head over the same paper that absorbed the other boys and join with them in prayer. Ivan wished the afternoon could go on forever.

It was Fyodor who had to leave first. They had finished their study and prayers, and were singing some of the church hymns their parents had taught them. Pyotr led enthusiastically.

As Fyodor prepared to leave, there was a flurry. Somehow Alexi had lost his paper with the Scripture among the empty glasses and plates on the table, or among the coats piled on the chairs. Fyodor helped to look for it as long as he could, but finally, cramming his gloves into his pockets and leaving his coat unbuttoned in his haste, he left with hurried apologies and more birthday wishes.

It was pleasant for the three other boys to sit together discussing school and their teachers and the ice hockey teams. Pyotr and Alexi thought Ivan should not worry about Boris and his threats. The coach had already shown that he wanted to overlook the fact that Ivan was not a member of the Young Pioneers. That should reassure him. And besides, Ivan was a very good player! Pyotr rumpled Ivan's hair affectionately. And it should not be too hard to stay away from Boris after school.

All too soon, the time came for Ivan to go home. Pyotr had been invited to stay for supper with Alexi, and was already singing loudly as he began to help clear up the room before Alexi's parents returned from church. Ivan shrugged into his coat reluctantly. It had been a wonderful afternoon. His heart sang as he ran lightly down the building's stairway to the front door.

If he had known what was waiting for him, he would not have been whistling as he opened the door and stepped out into the darkening street.

Police
questioning

Ivan was intent on peering down the road to see if a bus was coming through the freezing Moscow twilight. At first he did not notice the two men moving out of a doorway towards him.

He began to run as the dim lights of the bus appeared, the cold snow creaking and snapping under his boots.

'Ivan Nazaroff?' Ivan was startled as the two figures squarely blocked his way. In an instant he knew they were members of the secret police. His heart pounded.

'Yes?' How could they know his name?

'Where are you coming from?'

Ivan's tongue seemed frozen in his mouth. The bus lumbered slowly past him, its headlights catching the three figures by the edge of the street, then moving on.

The taller of the two men, a disciplined, soldierlike figure, took Ivan's arm. 'I am Comrade Grigory Yakov. You have some questions to answer, Ivan Nazaroff. We will go to the police station and see what we can discover.'

Squeezed between the two officers in the back seat of the small police car, Ivan stared at the seat in front of him. He did not dare turn his head to look out of the wide windows. The tall policeman was sitting erect, glancing at his watch and out into the winter evening.

The other officer had leaned his head against his window and appeared to be falling asleep. The driver of the car never turned to look at his passengers.

Ivan clenched his hands together in his lap in an effort to gather strength for what lay ahead. If only Dad were with him! He pictured the scene at home: Katya setting the table and Mum bringing in the plates of bread and soup, perhaps glancing out the window to see if he were coming.

With eyes open, Ivan began to pray. It was hard to concentrate in the lurching car, as it slowed for intersections and then sped up. Ivan was anxious not to appear to be praying. He tried to tighten the muscles in his face into a stern expression.

The car slid to a quiet stop. Comrade Yakov sprang out, holding the door for Ivan. The three walked briskly through the iron entrance gates and into the bright light of the police station. They entered a small room where the men began removing their coats. Ivan took his coat off as he was directed, hands shaking as he unbuttoned his coat.

Comrade Yakov sat down behind a small desk, pen in hand.

'Comrade Ivan Nazaroff, where were you this afternoon?' His voice was patient and not unfriendly.

'At a birthday party. At the home of Alexi Petrovich. I've done nothing wrong.'

The second officer lazily lit a cigarette and stood in front of Ivan. 'Yes. You were at the home of Alexi Petrovich. Perhaps it was his birthday. Perhaps it was something else, as well.' He blew a puff of smoke towards the ceiling. 'What did you do at the home of Alexi Petrovich?'

'We had a birthday party. We had tea and biscuits

that my mother sent, and cakes.' It helped to be able to talk.

'And who else was at this home this afternoon?' The first officer raised his pen.

'It was a birthday party. Alexi Petrovich, my friend, was fourteen.'

'Who else was present?' Comrade Yakov frowned. He did not like to repeat himself.

Ivan sat staring at the pen in Comrade Yakov's hand. If it were only a birthday party, why would he not tell the names of those present? To refuse would be to admit that something illegal had taken place. In a low voice he gave the names of his friends, insisting, 'It was a birthday party.'

But the interrogation was just beginning. A long line of questions followed, concerning his school, his father's job, his mother's job, the name of every friend he could remember, where his family had lived before coming to their present flat, his teacher's name, his grades, his sister's grades, her friends. Ivan began to feel light-headed from the stuffy room and from hunger. He had not eaten supper, even if the police had. Did Ivan have a Bible? Did he know what Jeremiah meant? Did he ever attend church?

It seemed that hours had passed, when the two men abruptly stood and left, locking the door of the small room behind them without explanation. As the door quickly opened and closed for the men, Ivan's heart lurched. He thought he glimpsed a boy in the hall – perhaps two boys.

After a long interval, the officers returned. They appeared pleased; there was a lightness in their manner, although their faces remained professionally severe.

35

More questions followed, this time along a different and more alarming line.

Was it possible that his father was religious? What prayer-house* did his father attend? Was his mother a believer? Was he? His sister? The answers burned in his throat and he could feel trickles of perspiration down the sides of his face. Again the questions returned to the birthday party, and Ivan repeated the answers he had given earlier. There was a pause. Putting his hand inside his pocket, Comrade Yakov slowly pulled out the small piece of paper on which Alexi had written his verses from Jeremiah.

Ignoring the paper, and asking the questions as if he did not know the answer, Comrade Yakov leaned towards Ivan. 'At this "birthday party", a paper was passed around. What was on the paper?'

Ivan's eyes reflected his horror at seeing the white paper in the officer's hand. Angrily, Comrade Yakov shouted the question again.

'Verses from Jeremiah.' What would happen to him? He knew of older Christian boys who had been beaten by the police.

'What is that? What is Jeremiah?' The short officer was smoking again, and he spat out his words.

Suddenly Ivan could almost see his father as he looked when he came home from his interview at the police station only days earlier. Ivan remembered his words: 'It is an honour to suffer for his sake.' Ivan took a steadying breath.

'It is a part of the Bible, comrade. It is a part of the Old Testament.'

There was a long pause. There was a stillness in the room that had not been there before. *Perhaps it is my*

* Soviet term for church building.

36

own fears that are still, Ivan thought. He had stopped trembling, and he raised a hand to push his wet hair off his forehead.

'That is all for the present. You may go home now.' Comrade Yakov's voice seemed to boom out of a vacuum. Ivan could not believe what he was hearing. But the police left immediately, leaving the door open behind them as their footsteps rapidly faded down the hall.

A cold blast of air from the corridor made Ivan begin to shake. Quickly he pulled on his coat. The hall was dark and empty, and he hurried outside. From the appearance of the streets, Ivan knew it was late. Knees still shaking from his ordeal, he found his way to an underground station entrance, grateful that he still had his bus fare in his coat pocket. An old woman swabbing the underground platform with a filthy mop glanced at him in surprise. Ivan was sure, then, that it was very late.

Pyotr's
accusal

It seemed strange that life continued in the ordinary way the next day. The evening at the police station had been so extraordinary that somehow Ivan was surprised that the streets of Moscow were unchanged and that the hours at school passed as if nothing had happened to him at all.

Returning home so late the night before and seeing every window in his parents' flat lit in the darkened building had given Ivan a peculiar sensation. Such a feeling of exhaustion had overcome him that it had been hard to force himself up the stairs, even though he was longing for food and bed and was eager to relieve his family's fears.

But today, in spite of an odd feeling of tiredness, all seemed as before.

Perhaps it was because Ivan was dozing over his homework after school that he was so startled by Dad's unusually early homecoming from work. Dad seemed suddenly to be in the room, the door still opened behind him. He laughed at their astonishment, swinging Katya in his arms and making her shriek with delight. He set Katya down and gave Mum a joyful hug. Bewildered, Ivan closed the door. His mind was hazy with sleep, but he knew it was much too soon for Dad to be home from the collective farm.

Gathering the family to the table, Dad laughed away their excited questions and began to explain. 'This morning at the train station, as I was waiting to go to the farm with the other workers, a police car pulled up and the comrade officer called me over.'

Ivan saw his mother's folded hands tighten.

'I was told to get in to be driven to the underground, where I could get transportation to my factory! I was told to return to my old job at the factory, and that is where I have worked all day.'

Mum's eyes were wet. 'Praise to our glorious God!'

'Yes!'

Smiles of joy remained on the family's faces throughout the evening. Katya finished her homework early enough to read a book before bedtime. Apparently all was well with the world.

Ivan tried not to think about the questions that were nagging at his brain. *Why was Dad given his job back?* There was something about it that did not seem to fit. He tried to concentrate on his homework, but his train of thought was often interrupted by a flood of questions. All day he had watched at school for Alexi or Pyotr or Fyodor. He was worried that he had not seen any of them all day. *Were they not at school? Were they being held by the police? How had the police known about the meeting? How had they obtained the paper with the Bible verses?* His head swam and buzzed over his books, and then everything was quiet. From a long distance away he could hear Mum's voice.

'Ivan. No more homework! You must go to bed. You had so little sleep last night!' Dad was helping him up from his chair and leading him to bed. Almost in a dream, he undressed and fell asleep.

Snow fell all the next day. The students in Moscow School Number 17 were accustomed to seeing it pile up on the sills of the narrow windows until it almost blocked their view of the sky. Ivan tried to shake off the questions that had worried him. Last night's sleep had greatly refreshed him, and the events of the Sunday night police questioning seemed unreal. Perhaps nothing more would come of it. Still, Ivan's eyes scanned the halls and courtyards for a glimpse of one of his Christian friends.

Sophia Kutskova praised Ivan as he gathered up his books for the day and slipped them into his schoolbag.

'I am happy to see you working so hard, Ivan.' She smiled, her eyes resting on the collar of his shirt. He knew she was silently reminding him that he ought to be wearing the red neck scarf of the Young Pioneers.

'There is to be an all-Moscow intermediate history competition in the spring. Examinations will be given, and students with the best marks from all the schools will be asked to write a historical essay. You have the highest grade in our classroom, Ivan. I would like to choose you to represent our class, and indeed, the intermediate school.' She hesitated. 'Of course, I cannot select a student of history who does not proudly wear his own country's red scarf.' There was a pleading in her eyes that made Ivan uncomfortable. 'You could win for our school, Ivan. I know it. Over every other school in Moscow! Please think about what I am saying.'

Ivan hurried along the hall. In a group of students ahead, Katya was chatting with a classmate. Ivan knew she would be so happy to have a friend that she would not want to ride on the bus with him.

Outside, the wind stung his face, and he licked the snowflakes that fell on his lips. Some boys were sliding on the ice in the schoolyard, while others were throwing huge snowballs and shouting with laughter as the snowballs exploded softly on the coats of their classmates. Ivan heard his name called. It was Pyotr, pushing between students, his breath puffing a cloud in front of him as he ran, and his blond hair wet against his forehead.

A handful of snow Pyotr had scooped up as he ran hit Ivan softly on the chest, bursting in all directions in a spray of white.

'You want a snowball fight, do you, Pyotr Kachenko?' Ivan called with joy. Pyotr was beside him now, catching his breath and frowning. His voice was guarded.

'Stay over here a bit, away from the others. Keep the snowballs coming. I want to talk to you.'

It would be safer, of course, if they were not seen together for too long. Pretending to have a snowball fight was a good idea, but Pyotr looked very upset as he told Ivan what had happened.

All the boys from Alexi's party had been taken that Sunday night to the police station. All had been questioned and finally released, Pyotr reported. Fines of fifty rubles each had been assigned to the parents of the boys, for permitting them to attend an 'illegal youth meeting'.

Ivan wondered why his parents had not been fined. Fifty rubles! That was a lot of money!

Pyotr was indignant about the paper with the verses from Jeremiah. How had the police obtained this? Ivan also wondered.

In a flash, his head seemed to clear. He understood

the uneasy questions that had been nagging him since Sunday. An informer! One of the boys would have to have told!

He could hardly bring himself to put the thought into words. Catching a gloveful of snow and tossing it, he stepped a little closer to Pyotr.

'Could there have been – an informer, Pyotr?'

Pyotr's expression did not change. He crossed his arms and thrust out his chin, observing Ivan carefully.

'I was going to ask you that question, Ivan.'

Ivan stared in dismay at the accusing face of his friend.

He, the informer? Surely Pyotr couldn't think that he would do such a thing! Suddenly he felt as if he were with a stranger. He stammered as he spoke.

'But, Pyotr! You don't think it was *me*? Why – why would I do such a thing?'

The older boy's face remained unchanged. 'I wonder how many rubles *your* family had to pay, Ivan.' Seeing Ivan's confused expression, he continued sadly, 'You told us on Sunday that your father had lost his job at the factory and had to do unskilled labour at the state collective farm. Yet everyone knows that now he has his old job back. Why would such a nice thing happen to your father, Ivan?'

Ivan could not bear the hurt expression on Pyotr's face. His eyes dropped to the snow at his feet as he answered, 'I do not know, Pyotr Kachenko. But I promise you, it had nothing to do with me. You must not think I was the informer.'

But the boots of Pyotr Kachenko were already moving swiftly away from Ivan. Pyotr had not waited for an answer.

A
frightening
visit

It would have been easier if Ivan had told his parents about Pyotr's accusation.

It would have been better, perhaps, but Ivan decided not to do it. His parents had enough worries of their own.

But it was hard. Only for an hour or two every day did Ivan forget that his friends believed he was an informer. Bent over his hockey stick, skimming the ice, slamming the puck to his teammates, Ivan thought of nothing except the game, the net, and the score. It was wonderful to have been chosen for the team, and an admiring glance from a teammate as he shot the puck or a word of encouragement from the coach pushed him into playing as never before.

Boris Petrovich was a brilliant goalie, moving constantly, crouching in the net, swaying from side to side, his eyes never leaving the puck. Soon the league games would begin. Boris was sure to be chosen. So far Boris had not made an issue of the fact that, as a Christian, Ivan belonged to no communist organisation. But when the league games sponsored by the Komsomol began, would he then begin to complain?

In the locker room, Ivan watched him move from friend to friend, laughing, and making his way to the coach to tell some joke that brought an amused smile to the lips of the older man. Every other member of the school team was also a member of the Young Pioneers, or had just turned fifteen and joined the Komsomol. They knew each other well from the club meetings, and Ivan envied the boys' easy friendliness with one another. He threw his skates in his locker and quietly made his way out of the locker room and into the biting Moscow cold.

It seemed a long time since he had seen Alexi or Fyodor. He did not blame them for avoiding him, if they thought he was an informer. They had to be cautious. Their families had already been heavily fined. Why would they continue to be friends with a person whom they thought had informed?

The wind wailed between the buildings. Ivan felt miserably alone. He had to tell someone!

Katya was curled up in Dad's chair reading her geography notes. She was trying to memorise the major cities of the Ural mountains, and she barely looked up as Ivan flung himself into the apartment.

'Katya!'

She lowered her book, surprised by the urgent note in Ivan's voice.

'I've got to talk to you! I'm in trouble.'

Katya's half smile faded into concern. She uncurled her legs and sat on the edge of Dad's chair as Ivan drew up a wooden chair from the big table beside her.

'What trouble?'

'I can't tell Dad and Mum. They have enough troubles of their own. But something doesn't make sense.'

Katya strained to follow the conversation.

'Dad is fired from his job at the factory and told he must work as a farmer in the collective outside Moscow.' His voice was thoughtful. 'That Sunday I participate in a Christian meeting with my friends. Someone reports all of us. The next day, Dad has his job back at the factory, and we are not even fined, although the other boys' families are. I don't understand.'

Katya shook her head in impatience. '*I* don't understand what *trouble* you're in. Do you mean that questioning by the police?'

'No, it's not that . . .'

'Then what?'

Ivan still talked slowly, his eyes searching Katya's face for reactions.

'Someone informed. Right, Katya?'

'Yes!' Her voice was impatient.

'The boys think it was me,' his words came in a rush, 'so that Dad could get back his job at the factory. They think I went to the police and confessed and offered their names because of Dad.'

Katya's expression froze.

'Your friends told you they think *you* are an *informer*?' Her shock melted into anger. 'It's terrible that they could think such a thing!'

Ivan smiled at her loyalty. 'No. It is logical. There was no other way for the police to discover that we were studying Scripture except through an informer.' What he was saying suddenly chilled him to the bone. 'Katya! *I* am not the informer! But one of the other boys *is*!'

The children sat in silence for a moment. The enormity of the idea overwhelmed them.

'The police had been given the piece of paper with Scripture on it that we used at the meeting. It had to be someone who had been there. Katya, I've been so upset about being accused of informing, I've not wanted to face the fact that the real informer has to be Pyotr, Fyodor, or Alexi. But we have to admit this must be true.'

Katya looked bleak.

Ivan paced the floor impatiently. 'Don't you see? Everyone thinks I am the informer, so they will be careful about me. They hardly speak to me. But the real informer can keep on passing along more information to the police.'

'Oh, Ivan! Tell Dad! I'm scared.'

Ivan paced restlessly to the window and back, unable to keep his body still while his mind was in an uproar. In less than an hour, Mum would be home. Ivan was thankful that there was that much time before she was to arrive. He glanced out at the street as if to assure himself that she was not coming. What he saw drained the colour out of his face.

'Katya!' His heart was pounding. 'Sit down and pretend to do your homework.'

Katya's eyes widened nervously.

'The police who questioned me last Sunday are turning into our building.'

Katya gasped.

'They may not be coming here. Katya, you must not look afraid.'

There was a loud pounding on the door.

The two officers looked exactly as they had before. Their eyes swept the small flat as they entered. No, it did not matter that the parents were not yet home from work. It was Ivan to whom they wished to speak. It would be convenient perhaps, for little sister to wait in another room? This did not concern her.

Ivan admired Katya's dignity as she picked up her

notes and went into the bedroom, closing the door behind her with a respectful smile at the police. He could imagine how she would be sitting, trembling, on the bed. He knew she was praying.

As the police talked, Ivan was astonished that they knew he was suspected by his friends of being an informer. And they had been at school checking his grades. How Sophia Kutskova would have assured them she was doing everything she could to draw Ivan away from the superstition of his parents!

Comrade Lutsgov's voice remained friendly.

'I see from your school records you are following our great leader Lenin's advice when he said, "Study, study, and study!"'

'Yes, comrade.' Ivan felt uncomfortable.

'You do follow the teachings of Lenin, then?'

'Some of them. You know I am a Christian.' Lenin, like Marx, had said, 'Religion is the opiate of the people.'

The short officer sighed impatiently. 'We do not think this childish faith of yours will last long. We have already written down your name in a police file. Think of it, young comrade. You are just a boy, and yet your name is with those who resist the glorious new world our leader Lenin called us to.'

Comrade Yakov put an arm around Ivan's shoulders. Ivan tried not to stiffen. 'It is not too late for you, Ivan Nazaroff. We need intelligent boys like you to serve Mother Russia. We can see to it, Ivan, that you can play ice hockey on any Soviet teams you're good enough for.' Ivan's heart lurched. 'But I think it is history, also, that you love. We can give you entrance to Moscow University, in years to come, if you will put aside this foolish

Christian fable and help us. You could become a great historian someday.'

Ivan was torn between wishing his mother would come home and fearing that the door would open and she *would* be there.

'Don't you want to continue your education?'

Ivan swallowed. 'Yes, comrade. With all my heart.'

'But you know very well it will be almost impossible for you to go to university if you are not a member of the Young Communist League.'

'But I cannot join.' Ivan hoped he sounded respectful.

'Of course you can.' Yakov drew him to the settee, and together they sat down. The short officer stood by the window, watching the street.

'That is why we are here. You can stay within your group of believers. Go to little meetings like last Sunday's, as before. From time to time, answer some questions for us about the other believers. You will not have to join the Communist party openly. You will nobly serve our glorious motherland. Ivan, already your "Christian" friends have turned against you.'

The second officer turned from the window, smiling. 'We can see to it that they will no longer believe that you are the informer. It would be necessary to remove that impression!'

'How could you do that?'

'How?' The officer chuckled good-naturedly. 'By letting it leak out who the real informer is. Those things are easily arranged.'

It would be a truly wonderful thing, Ivan thought, no longer to be suspected. And for the real informer to be found out! The whole church would be safer then.

Comrade Yakov sighed. 'If we were not concerned

for you, Ivan Nazaroff, if we did not care about your future, why would we come here? You are our young comrade. A great future can be yours. We are extending to you the hand of brotherhood. Join us!'

Ambush

They had given him a week to decide. Ivan tossed on his bed night after night, his mind a storm of thoughts. Perhaps he could pretend to cooperate with the police. Then the real informer would be exposed as they promised. It might be that he could give worthless information to the police. But could he? They would find out. What would happen to him then?

Walking to school, Ivan imagined his coming meeting with the police. If he refused, what would they do? A cold fear swept over him.

And how would he ever become free from the label of *informer*? One of the other boys was guilty, perhaps every day giving information to the police without any fear of suspicion. Ivan couldn't imagine any of his friends doing such a thing. But it had been done!

Ivan had been glad for the thick door between the living room and bedroom. If Katya had heard the police asking him to inform, she would have immediately told their parents when they returned from work. As it was, he had enough trouble persuading her that nothing would be gained by worrying Mum and Dad about a second questioning.

It was a Christian shortwave programme that gave Ivan direction. The radio preacher had been talking about a man, Daniel, who was sentenced to death in a den of many hungry lions. Daniel had refused to obey the wrong laws of his government.

But God had not let Daniel be harmed. By a miracle, he had closed the jaws of the lions, and Daniel had not been eaten. Ivan listened closely.

'I am innocent before God,' Daniel had declared to his king. That was why he had been safe from the lions. God had protected him.

Would God protect me from the anger of the police if I refused to inform? Ivan wondered to himself. The radio pastor continued with his sermon, but Ivan was left behind in his thoughts. Quietly a *yes* seemed to grow within him. God *would* protect him! His spirit lifted in a freedom he had not felt for a long time.

But God had not spoken to him about Sophia Kutskova, Ivan thought grimly, as he recopied a history chart for his teacher. Nothing he could do these days seemed to satisfy her. She had not mentioned to him that the police had asked her questions about Ivan. But her impatience with him seemed to grow day by day. She began to make teasing remarks to the class about Ivan's Christianity. She had never done this before.

Today she was angry. Why could Ivan not understand the most simple directions? Perhaps all the religion he had collected into his head was festering there and making ordinary thoughts impossible. A ripple of laughter passed over the class. Ivan stared at his desk, his face red from embarrassment.

Later she stood next to his desk, speaking to the class in a grieved tone. 'Ivan does not wish to represent our school in the all-Moscow history contest.' Helpless, Ivan sat with his head lowered, desperately fighting back tears of disappointment and frustration at the news. 'Perhaps, if he wanted, he could win for us. But such things do not interest him, I am afraid. It may be that he is too busy praying to God to work on such an earthly thing as a history essay for the honour of his school.' Ivan could feel the disgusted glances of his classmates.

It was hard to have his hopes dashed so suddenly. He had been secretly dreaming that Sophia Kutskova would permit him to enter an essay in the contest, even if he were not a member of the Young Pioneers. There were no official rules against it. Of course, if he should win, his victory would be difficult for the Soviet public to understand. How could an uninformed Christian fanatic win a Russian history contest? But all the same, Ivan thought, she did not have to pretend to the class that he had refused.

But it seemed that all friendliness with his teacher was over. When her eyes met Ivan's gaze, she hardened her expression.

In the past, it had not been difficult to overlook the small spites of some of his classmates – his pencil deliberately broken if he left his seat or a foot stuck suddenly in the aisle as he walked to the chalkboard.

But today everything seemed to be going wrong. Vladimir Covich had given him a violent shove as the class stood for Sophia Kutskova's entrance into the room. Ivan had lurched forward, almost falling on his desk and hitting his side on its sharp corner. His muscles tensed with pain.

As the class seated itself, Vladimir had whispered, 'Aren't you supposed to bless me, Christian?'

Later, as Ivan stood in turn to recite for his teacher, someone had quietly lifted his inkwell from its place on his desk and poured a thin trickle of ink across his notebook. Ivan was certain Sophia Kutskova had seen it happening. How could she not have seen? But she had said nothing. Ivan had to stay in the classroom during his lunch hour to recopy his ink-smeared work. His stomach growled with hunger.

By late afternoon, Ivan felt he was sick. He had a headache, and he could hardly force himself to do his work. He was afraid to raise his eyes from his desk and encounter the hard look of his teacher. His side ached.

Somehow it was Sophia Kutskova's fault. Her taunting him these last few days had seemed to unleash in the class a spirit of hostility against Ivan that had never existed before. As the last bell rang, tears of relief sprang to his eyes. He was ashamed of how close to tears he had been all day.

There would be no waiting for Katya today. Ivan was going home, far away from school, as fast as he could. His heavy boots kicked a small spray of snow as he walked. Each step was that much farther from the school. Abruptly he stopped, his way blocked by Vladimir Covich and several other classmates.

'Ivan Nazaroff?' Someone behind him called his name commandingly. Swiftly Ivan turned his head, and immediately felt a sharp blow on his temple. A look of astonishment spread over his face, and then one of pain as he was hit hard in the stomach and on the jaw at the same time. Books flying, he skidded in the slippery snow and awkwardly tried to regain his balance.

'You need to learn a lesson, Nazaroff.' There seemed to be a voice close to his ear. 'You need to learn that we won't put up with you forever!' With the next blow, Ivan was down in the snow. A warm trickle of blood caught in his eyelashes and smeared his cheeks. The boys were on top of him, delivering blow upon blow. Ivan

felt as if he were suffocating with pain and fear. He coughed and cried and struggled against the weight of bodies and the flailing arms and fists. His head swam in blackness.

Discovery!

Pyotr's voice was coming from a long way off. He was calling insistently, but Ivan was too tired to answer. He wanted only to be left to sleep. But the calling continued. Ivan would have to answer. He was gathering strength to respond, when he realised Pyotr was not calling him. He was calling Fyodor. Gratefully, Ivan sank back into oblivion, only to be roused by a hand gently shaking his shoulder.

'Ivan! Ivan! Get up!' The voice had been calling him after all. He felt himself being pulled to his feet. Far-off pain made him open his eyes in bewilderment. The pain seemed to be spinning ever closer, like a hot meteor falling from the sky. Ivan groaned suddenly, as the meteor seemed to crash into his head.

'We'll help you, Ivan.' Pyotr's voice was filled with concern. 'Can you walk?'

Ivan tried to answer. His mouth felt huge and unworkable. Finally he groaned an assent, the pain pounding at him as if it wanted release.

'What is this? You have been fighting, Ivan?' Sophia Kutskova was out of breath, as if she had been running. 'You have been fighting, Ivan?'

'Sophia Kutskova, we just now found Ivan in the snow.'

'It looks as if he got the worst of the fight,' the teacher replied coolly. 'Such conduct is not permitted, as Ivan knows. Bring him to the principal.' She turned and slowly led the way back into the school and along the first floor corridor to the principal's office.

'I can walk alone,' Ivan gasped to Pyotr. 'Tell Sophia Kutskova I don't need help.' He was feeling better, except for the hammering in his head.

The principal invited him to sit down, and Ivan felt a surge of gratitude as he carefully lowered himself into the chair. Sophia Kutskova and the principal were talking quietly on the other side of the room. Finally the principal returned and looked sternly at Ivan. It was unfortunate that such a thing had occurred. The principal regretted that any students at Moscow School Number 17 would choose such unpeaceful methods of settling disputes. He would not ask Ivan to report the names of the other boys. But clearly, Ivan had been fighting. He would have to be punished. A week's suspension from school was decided upon, and Ivan was directed to return home immediately. This incident, along with other things (the principal glanced sympathetically at Sophia Kutskova) would go on Ivan's record. The principal hoped that a week's absence from school would give Ivan time to think about his conduct and resolve to improve.

The bus ride home, with every movement of the vehicle shooting stabs of pain through Ivan's head and legs, the curious stares of people on the street – all seemed part of a dream to Ivan. Even the shock on his mother's face, the speed with which she eased him into bed, and the cool cloths on his head and hot towels on his aching legs seemed unreal.

There was something bothering Ivan, something that

kept emerging from the pain in his head. It was not the beating. Such things had happened to others before, and pain would go away. He remembered Pyotr's voice coming from a long distance. 'Ivan! Ivan! Get up.' That was not it.

In a rush, Ivan was in the schoolyard again, throwing snowballs at Pyotr. Pyotr's eyes had been unfriendly that day, too. It was Pyotr saying, 'If you are not the informer, Ivan, why would your father be given his old job back?' It was the look of sadness on Pyotr's face!

To Sophia Kutskova and his classmates, Ivan was an outsider. Now, to his old friends, Alexi, Fyodor, and Pyotr, he was an outsider because they thought him to be an informer. Loneliness far worse than the pain swept over him. The informer had to be found! He closed his eyes in a haze of hurt.

It seemed only a moment later that Mum was gently bathing his swollen face in warm water. She was dressed for work. Dad had already left, and Katya was hovering behind Mum, her eyes rimmed with red. Ivan could not think why Katya had been crying.

'Praise to the Lord,' Mum was saying with a soft smile. 'You slept all night, Ivan. I'm sorry to wake you, but Katya and I must leave soon.'

A small tray with porridge and tea was on the table by his bed. Ivan tried to sit up. Pain in his shoulders and legs pushed him back against his pillow.

Katya gave a rueful smile. 'To think the principal suspended you for a week, Ivan! As if you were not too injured to return!'

Mum was gently spooning porridge into Ivan's mouth. He shook his head and made another effort to lean on his arm. In his free hand he took the spoon and tried to swallow the cooled porridge. To please Mum, he

drank some tea. She and Katya helped him to sit on the edge of the bed and finish the tea.

Ivan knew Mum wanted to stay home with him. But how could she explain such an absence at work? And Katya must go to school as usual. Enough attention had already been brought to the Nazaroff family.

The days at home passed very slowly. In the evenings, Ivan tried to respond cheerfully to the family's kind and affectionate attentions.

But at night, when the lights were out and Ivan lay restlessly on his bed, or during the long days when he was alone in the flat, the problem of the informer's identity haunted him.

The answer came one evening as he was lying on the settee in the living room. His muscles were still sore and his head ached if he moved rapidly, but he had spent the day working on his schoolwork (or at least what he imagined his classmates might be doing) and had felt well. He had not spent time turning over and over in his mind the question of the informer. It was as if he had used up his quota of mental energy on that problem, and any attempt to return to it was met with a wall of mental rejection.

Their parents were visiting friends in the block of flats and Katya was pouring some tea she had made. Ivan sat up so suddenly he made Katya spill the tea.

'Katya! It just came to me! I know who the informer is!' Instead of protesting about the spilled tea, Katya stared at him excitedly.

'Ivan! Who?' The pool of tea on the tray cloth was slowly growing larger and larger. For the moment, Katya was unconcerned.

'Katya! It's so simple! Listen!' Ivan swung his stiff legs off the settee and leaned towards his sister.

'First, Fyodor left Alexi's house and was picked up by the police. Later, I left, and they were waiting for me. Pyotr stayed for supper at Alexi's and then the police got him. They got Alexi last, after all had gone.'

'I know all that !' Katya looked as if she would jump up and shake the information out of Ivan if he did not continue.

'But – ' Ivan's voice lifted over his sister's, 'when the police picked me up, they already had the paper with Scripture on it, and they knew that we had not simply been having a birthday party. They didn't bring the paper out until all the boys had been brought to the police station, but when they questioned me, they asked me if I knew what Jeremiah meant. They already had the paper before they questioned me !'

Katya's eyes were shocked. 'That means Fyodor – '

'Yes ! But *I'm* the only one who could know that for sure, because when you figure it out, the informer had to be either Fyodor or me, and it was not me !'

'You must tell Mum and Dad.'

Ivan felt a pang of regret at telling Katya. 'No ! It wouldn't do any good. They don't know that my friends think I am an informer. Knowing would only worry them, and they would be as helpless as you or I in trying to take the blame off me.'

Besides, something more was looming in Ivan's mind. In two days, he would have to return to the police station and give them his answer. This was a battle he had to fight alone.

In the lions' den

Perhaps he had made a mistake in not telling Katya he had to return to the police station. The crowd of students was thinning along the edges of the schoolyard, and a feeling of alarm came over Ivan. What if the police kept him for a long time? Katya was his link with home, and he was letting her slip away!

'Katya!' He could see her waiting in a long queue at the bus stop. She turned her head, pleased that he was looking for her. His feet flew along the pavement, skilfully avoiding bumping into people as he ran. Fear that the bus would whisk her away gave speed to his still aching legs.

She made a place for him in the queue. 'It's so crowded today, you would think it was a holiday. Such long queues for the buses!'

Ivan was in a fever of impatience. 'Katya! Listen. I have to go back to the police station for a little while.'

His voice was low, but he could not resist a nervous glance over his shoulder. No one seemed to have heard.

Katya was frightened. 'Ivan! What for? What has happened?'

'Nothing. Just listen. If I am late, you will know where I am. All right?' He turned swiftly.

'But wait, Ivan! Wait!' Katya could not leave her

place in the long queue to chase him for an answer. Gratefully, Ivan strode away. As he walked, he began to think about the radio sermon on Daniel in the lions' den.

It took him longer than he had expected to reach the police station. The streets were unusually full of people as he made his way through them, glad that he wasn't on the packed buses lurching by.

The iron gate of the police station clanged behind him with a grating sound that reminded Ivan uncomfortably of prison cells. But there was nothing to be nervous about. A simple matter. He had only to tell the police captain that he did not wish to be an informer. He had done nothing wrong. But all the same, his heart began pounding wildly as he approached the reception desk of the police station.

The officer was writing rapidly. A phone was ringing. People were coming and going at a fast pace. Ivan's eyes strayed to a guard at the head of a corridor, whose drab green uniform was almost grey in the shadow. Slung over his shoulder, his rifle glinted in the pale electric light.

Finally the comrade officer at the desk lifted his eyes to Ivan. He looked annoyed.

'What is it, young comrade? We are busy today.'

At that moment, Comrade Yakov stepped out of a room into the dim corridor and hurried to the front desk with a sheaf of papers.

'I have an appointment with him – with Comrade Yakov.' Ivan looked appealingly at the officer, waiting to be recognised.

Yakov groaned. 'I have no time today.'

Ivan's heart leaped with joy. So the Lord would shut up this lion's mouth ! But the next moment his hopes fell just as suddenly, as the officer said, 'Never mind. Come to my office. Ah! What a day!'

Yakov stood at his desk looking at Ivan. His voice was impatient.

'Now, Ivan Nazaroff, you have had a week to think over my offer. Are you tired of your friends blaming you unjustly for being an informer? I would wish for them they could be of such a service to Mother Russia! Have you found out that the love that you believers talk about doesn't go very far?'

Ivan spoke carefully. 'I think, comrade, that there *is* real love among Christians, even though it doesn't seem – '

'No! It *doesn't* "seem"! But I am very busy this afternoon. Shall I simply assume, then, that an intelligent young man like you has decided to prove himself a good citizen, and as a result enjoy all the benefits of our glorious revolution?'

A car started suddenly in the street outside the window. Ivan paled. It had sounded, for a moment, like a lion's roar.

Taking a full breath, Ivan chose his words as carefully as possible.

'I am sorry, Comrade Officer. I cannot become an informer. And in truth, there would be nothing to tell you. Believers do nothing against the Soviet Union or against the laws of our country – '

Yakov growled in anger. A small nerve twitched in his cheek. 'Ivan Nazaroff, I do not have time this afternoon for this kind of talk. You have been given an unusual opportunity. Yet you spurn it. You were involved in an illegal meeting, yet no fine was placed upon your parents. We were willing to overlook what hap-

pened because of your age. Certainly we expect you to come to your senses – '

An officer in full uniform poked his head in the door and took in the scene. Comrade Yakov nodded as if in response to a command. The officer disappeared.

'You are making a very serious mistake.' He paused, apparently more irritated than ever at Ivan's silence. 'Today, of all days, I do not have time to discuss the fate of one stupid boy. Do you realise there has been a breakdown in our great Moscow underground system – something electrical – and the trains on one section have stopped? Transportation is critical. I am needed elsewhere. Yet you stand here and waste my time.'

A phone was ringing in the distance. Ivan could hear hurried voices. Comrade Yakov looked furious for a second, then barked, 'Go home!'

A joyful relief flooded Ivan.

'And go quickly, before I make you wait here all night.'

His steps clicked rapidly down the corridor. Ivan stood for a second in the dim afternoon light. His hands were still clenched nervously at his side. A slow smile spread over his face, as with a sudden happy movement he wound his woollen scarf round his neck. He made his way, hands in pockets, past the reception desk and the officer at the desk, now almost hidden by a commotion of milling people.

Even in the lions' den! Ivan was exulting as he made his way through the ever more congested streets. *Even in the lions' den, the Lord kept me safe.*

Arriving home, Ivan could at last tell his parents all about the troubles and doubts he had gone through in the past few days. His words tumbled out joyously as he told how good God had been to him.

What could one do but celebrate, Mum and Dad decided. It was a bad thing that Ivan had not told them about the police asking him to inform. This was too heavy a burden for a boy to bear alone. And going to the police station without telling them! What if something had happened?

Dad kept shaking his head in pleasure and praising God for the breakdown of the underground system.

'If the officer had not been so busy with the transportation problems, he might have kept you at the station for hours. Perhaps overnight. To think how the Lord protected you! To think how it was this day, and no other, that it happened that you had to go! Praises! Praises to God!'

Ivan felt almost as giddy as Katya, who was whirling about the flat, perching for a moment on a chair or on the settee and leaping up, hugging Ivan until he insisted he had had the last hug he would endure.

Later, as the family sat around the large table in the living room drinking steaming glasses of tea and eating bread and butter and Mum's homemade jam, they began to piece together the events of the past few weeks.

Dad spoke slowly with good humour.

'When I was reported at the factory, my records were studied. I think it was clear to the police that I had done nothing wrong and that the man who reported me was lying. But it was, after all, an opportunity to ask me questions and to show me that those who are Christians are not friends of the state.'

Katya choked on her bread. 'Even though you love our country and have served faithfully in the army!'

Dad shook a finger at her, smiling gently. 'Oh, that was very long ago, Katychka. That no longer counts.'

Mum took the story up. 'When you would not answer

questions about the other believers, it was thought that perhaps your son could be made useful.'

'Yes! The police thought that if they could make Ivan angry at being falsely accused of informing, he would give up his beliefs and even spy for them.'

Ivan felt a rather unpleasant sensation in realising he had been the centre of police attention. 'When the police discovered that I had been at a Bible study, they planned a way to encourage me to inform. By giving you back your old job at the factory, Dad, it would look as if I *had* informed, and the others would be suspicious of me.'

'Which is exactly what happened.' Katya was biting with enthusiasm into her second piece of bread and jam.

Mum smiled proudly. 'Except that you did not agree to inform for them, Ivan.'

'But there is something I do not understand.' Dad rubbed his head reflectively. 'Why did the police *want* Ivan to become an informer? If Fyodor is an informer, as Ivan believes, there would be no need to have two to report on our group of believers.'

The family fell silent. It was a good question. But then, the ways of the police were past finding out.

A new
beginning

Now that the dreaded police interview was in the past,
Ivan wanted to start life afresh. After an examination in
school, one went the next day to a new section of
material, perhaps a new textbook. At least one began a
new page in one's notebook. It was satisfying to be able
to put the old behind, and to begin anew. But life was
not like that.

Unfortunately, Ivan was greatly behind in his work.
The week of suspension had resulted in Ivan's missing a
large amount of classwork. Sophia Kutskova offered
him no help in catching up. She ignored his return and
overlooked his raised hand in the question period following the lectures.

He wondered who had been chosen as the class candidate for the all-Moscow essay contest. Perhaps Sonya
Sorina. She was very good in history, Ivan knew.

In spare moments during the day, Ivan thought
about Fyodor betraying their small Bible study to the
police. It was very difficult to believe such a thing of
Fyodor. The boys and their families had been friends for
many years. Every spring Fyodor's family had gone
with Ivan's family to the Easter service in the forests
outside Moscow. Ivan was remembering Fyodor slush-

ing through the snowy mud, embarrassed by his too-large boots. How they had teased him!

His mother was a courageous woman. Once a week, in the evening after work, a small group of women gathered in her home under the pretence of an embroidery club. They would sit, needles flashing in the lamplight, singing hymns and sharing Bible verses and praying for one another.

It was difficult to believe Fyodor could have informed.

'Ivan Nazaroff?'

Ivan was trying to button his coat with one hand, holding his books in the other arm. He turned in surprise at the friendly tone. Sonya Sorina waited shyly, while the rest of the class streamed out of the room, happy to be gone.

'We get the same bus, Ivan. May I walk and talk with you?'

The crowded halls made talking impossible, and they walked together without trying to communicate until they were outside. Ivan glimpsed Alexi and Fyodor hurrying ahead of them. Fyodor cast a look over his shoulder at Ivan, then turned quickly back. Ivan was shocked at his face. Fyodor looked very tired. Perhaps sick.

Ivan's guess about Sonya had been correct. Sophia Kutskova had chosen her as the competition candidate. Sonya's red neck scarf had been caught in the collar of her coat when she put it on, and it seemed to point accusingly at Ivan.

She had been working on her essay, but she was concerned about it. It was against the contest rules for her to ask the advice of her teacher. But would Ivan read it?

She smiled hopefully as she stepped up into the bus ahead of him.

'Of course, Sonya!' Ivan smiled back eagerly. 'I am not sure that you need any help from me, but if you have your essay with you, I'll take it home and read it tonight.' Ivan was enjoying talking to a classmate again.

Sonya glanced quickly at Ivan, then down at her gloved hands in her lap. 'I'm sorry about what happened to you, Ivan. I mean the beating. It was cruel of the boys to do that, and you were very good not to tell on them. Many students in the class admire you for not telling and for not trying to pay them back.'

Ivan stared at Sonya in surprise. Could it be true that he had friends in the class? His voice was low. 'I thought that everyone was angry at me because I don't wear the red scarf and because I could not enter the contest.'

Sonya shook her head. 'Lenin himself said that there would be freedom of religion in Russia. I do not believe in any god, Ivan, but I know that it is not according to Lenin to be unjust to those who do. Others feel this way. You will see.'

That evening, Mum brought out her embroidery and sat at the table with Ivan and Katya as they did their homework. Dad was in his chair, listening to music on the radio and reading. It was a peaceful scene, and Ivan raced through page after page of homework, more industrious than he had been for a long time.

Mum's voice broke the silence. 'I was at Fyodor's house last evening. It was our Bible study.'

Katya's and Ivan's pens stopped in midsentence.

'I was telling the sisters about Ivan and how the

police had tried to persuade him to be an informer. And how he had refused.' Her eyes rested with a soft pride on Ivan's startled face. 'Why should I not tell?'

'But Fyodor's *mum*? You talked to her about informers?' Ivan marvelled.

'She does not know, Ivan, if Fyodor *did* inform on your Bible study at Alexi's. All the women rejoiced for you, Ivan, and so did I.'

Mum bent her head over her sewing, and said no more.

In later years, Ivan was to remember the next morning as a shower of white. Snow was falling as he stood on the cold floor by his bed, and the window was white with frost, with only the top of the pane clear enough for him to see the huge swirling flakes outside.

Mum had a simple white cloth on the breakfast table, and Katya's fresh face above her thick white sweater smiled over the bread and tea. The winter light in the room was bright.

They had all been surprised at the early pounding on the door. Dad had left for the factory, but Mum, who was getting ready to leave, pulled open the door in astonishment. Covered with a thick layer of light snow stood Alexi, Pyotr, and Fyodor, smiling shyly and asking to come in.

It was a few minutes before the boots were pulled off, the coats shaken in the hall, and the boys sitting at the table, glasses of amber tea warming their red fingers.

Katya sat dumbfounded at this unexpected visit, her eyes straying to Fyodor's face and moving away at the warning in her mother's eyes. There was laughing and what Katya called 'warming up talk' and then a stillness fell over the group.

74

Fyodor cleared his throat. He was looking at Ivan. 'I've come, Ivan, to tell you that I have done you a great wrong. I – I confessed this wrong to my family last night, and to the families of Pyotr Kachenko and Alexi Petrovich. They have forgiven me.'

He shifted in his chair. 'It was I who informed on the meeting at Alexi's. I permitted you to be blamed for it, and I was afraid to speak up. Although I didn't mean it, my silence led the police to try to make you an informer and caused you much suffering. I am asking a very great thing of you. I am asking you to forgive me.'

Many times Ivan had seen his father embrace a Christian friend. It was the Russian way. They would fling their outstretched arms around each other, slapping each other's backs, their faces wreathed in smiles.

In a moment he was on his feet. Seeing the smile on his face, Fyodor stood uncertainly by his chair. In a huge embrace, Ivan threw his arms around his friend. Never had Ivan felt so much like a Russian.

'Thank you, Fyodor! Thank you for telling me. All is well now.'

Fyodor tried to brush away the tears that were brimming in his eyes, as he continued.

'It was all an accident, from the very beginning. When I came out of Alexi's, the police picked me up. They knew about Mum's Bible studies and wanted to ask me questions. I thought that somehow they had found out about *our* meeting and were questioning me about that. When I got to the police station, I was confused trying to answer about the birthday party. What made everything worse was that the paper, with the verse of Scripture on it, was in my pocket with my gloves. I must have put my gloves on top of the paper and then picked it up with them and put the paper and

75

my gloves in my pocket together. To think of how we looked for it!'

Ivan began to laugh. Now that the problem was past, it all seemed amusing. Soon the boys and then Katya and Mum were laughing.

'When I was about to leave the police station, I took my gloves out of my pocket. Out fell the paper. The police read it and then made me take off my coat again. I had already told the names of those at the birthday party.'

'As I did,' Ivan assured him.

'So that is how it all came to be. After it happened, I was a coward not to tell the truth about it. But I made myself think it didn't matter. My parents will explain everything to the believers, Ivan. No one will think of you as an informer again.'

Alexi slapped Fyodor on the back. 'Nor are you an informer, Fyodor! It was not intended.'

'No! It was not.' Fyodor looked so fierce, Katya thought she would laugh again. 'They did try to make me agree to keep on bringing them information whenever I could, but I would not!'

'That's the part we couldn't understand,' Ivan declared. 'Why the police would want me to inform, when they already *had* an informer in our ranks.' He looked shyly at Fyodor. 'I knew it was you, Fyodor.'

'I thought you suspected, Ivan. You knew the informer was not you, and it had to be one of us. I have been so ashamed.'

Mum cleared away the glasses of tea as she spoke. 'It is a good life we believers have! We can always make a new beginning.'

'Yes! It is very good!' Ivan smiled in happiness at his

three friends. In a few moments they were making their way to school through the snowy streets. The world was white.